For Eleanor,
seven pounds, one ounce

E
479-9634

First US edition 2020
First published by Walker Books Ltd. (UK) 2020

Library of Congress Catalog Card Number pending
ISBN 978-1-5362-1113-9

CCP 25 24 23 22 21 20
10 9 8 7 6 5 4 3 2 1

Printed in Shenzhen, Guangdong, China

This book was typeset in Bembo Educational and TW Cen MT.
The illustrations were done in watercolor and ink.

Candlewick Press
99 Dover Street
Somerville, Massachusetts 02144

www.candlewick.com

Ellie's Dragon

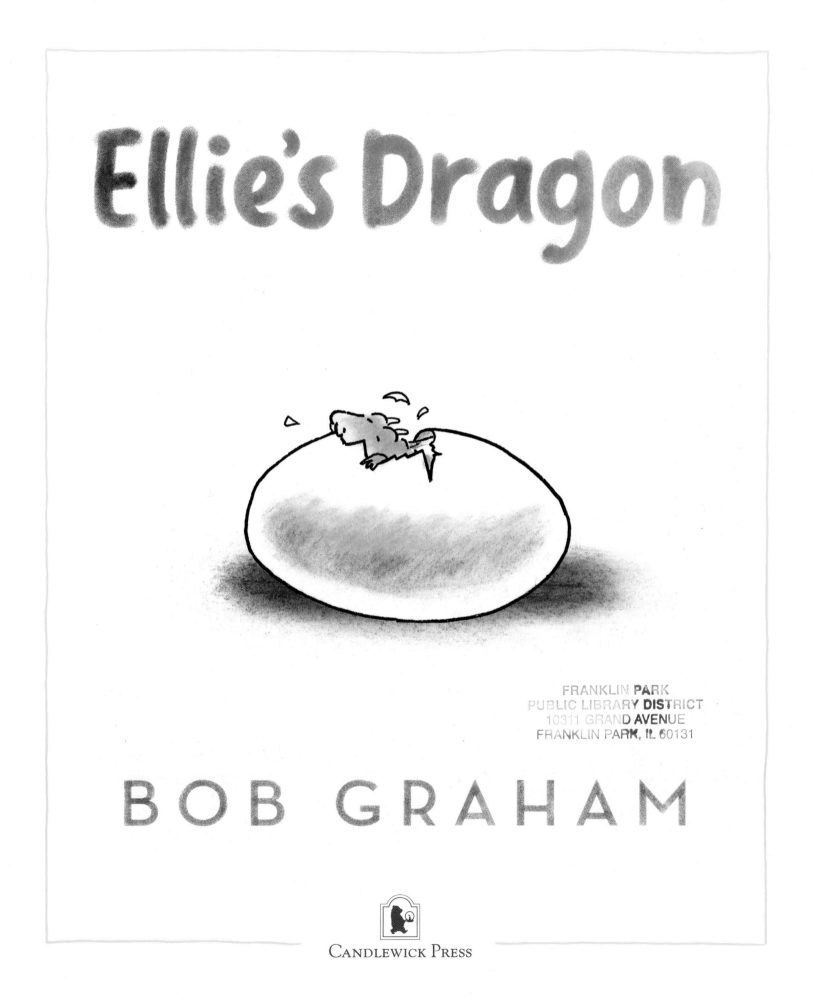

BOB GRAHAM

CANDLEWICK PRESS

When Ellie was quite young, she found a newborn dragon.
With its eyes not yet open, it crawled across an egg carton.
It was pale and luminous, with shifting
rainbow colors, like oil on water.

Its little claws tickled in the palm of Ellie's hand.
It was quite the sweetest thing she had ever seen.

She called
him Scratch.

At home, she made him a bed.
Scratch opened his eyes,
black as charcoal.

His tiny wings shivered; he was flightless as a silkworm.

"He wants some matches, Mommy.
He wants to eat the tops off."

"Certainly not!" replied her mom.
"You can't play with matches, sweetie."

Her mom saw nothing but an empty
matchbox and some cotton balls.

For a time, Scratch lived on the top floor of Ellie's dollhouse. She trained him to use the dragon litter box. Ellie fed her beast nasturtiums, chilis, burnt toast, and charcoal briquettes.

Ellie grew a little and went to preschool.

Ali saw him.

"He's sweet," he said.

Angie saw him, too.

"He's gorgeous," she said.

"Cool!" added
Amber and Luke.

But the
teacher
saw nothing.

Ellie grew some more.

She turned five and started kindergarten.

She was so excited that she forgot to take Scratch along.

It completely slipped her mind!

So Ellie didn't see her dragon's first flight . . .

which was
mainly downward.

Ellie had her eighth birthday.

Ali, Angie, and Luke were there.

While the candles were still smoking,

Scratch ate them.

And the same night, when all were asleep . . .

Scratch
flew!

Ellie's dad came on the
weekends to take her out.

He never knew he
had an extra passenger . . .

or that Ellie shared her popcorn.

Two years later, on Ellie's tenth birthday,
Angie, Luke, and Ali came for a sleepover.

But things were changing for Ellie and Scratch.

Ellie still loved her dragon.

But Scratch had way outgrown the dollhouse.

So had she.

Dragons breathe fire, dragons
breathe smoke, and dragons fly.
Dragons don't dance.
Scratch spent more time
dreaming on his fire blanket
in the corner.

Then Ellie was eleven,
and Scratch began to fade.

With the boom-boom-boom of the
Disco Poppy Girls in her ears,
Ellie could no longer hear the slow pump
of air under Scratch's wings.

The year after,
Ellie could see right through him.

On her thirteenth birthday, Scratch's breath
barely melted the icing on the cake.
He didn't even eat the candles.

And then he slipped quietly away into the night.

Occasionally, Ellie thought to look for him—and almost saw the flick of a tail from the corner of her eye.

She thought she smelled smoke—or heard a low fiery furnace over the fence.

But Scratch had not gone away. Little Sam found
him wandering down the street—

a fully grown, house-trained, affectionate dragon,
just looking for a new home.

And Scratch will probably live
with him for some time to come.

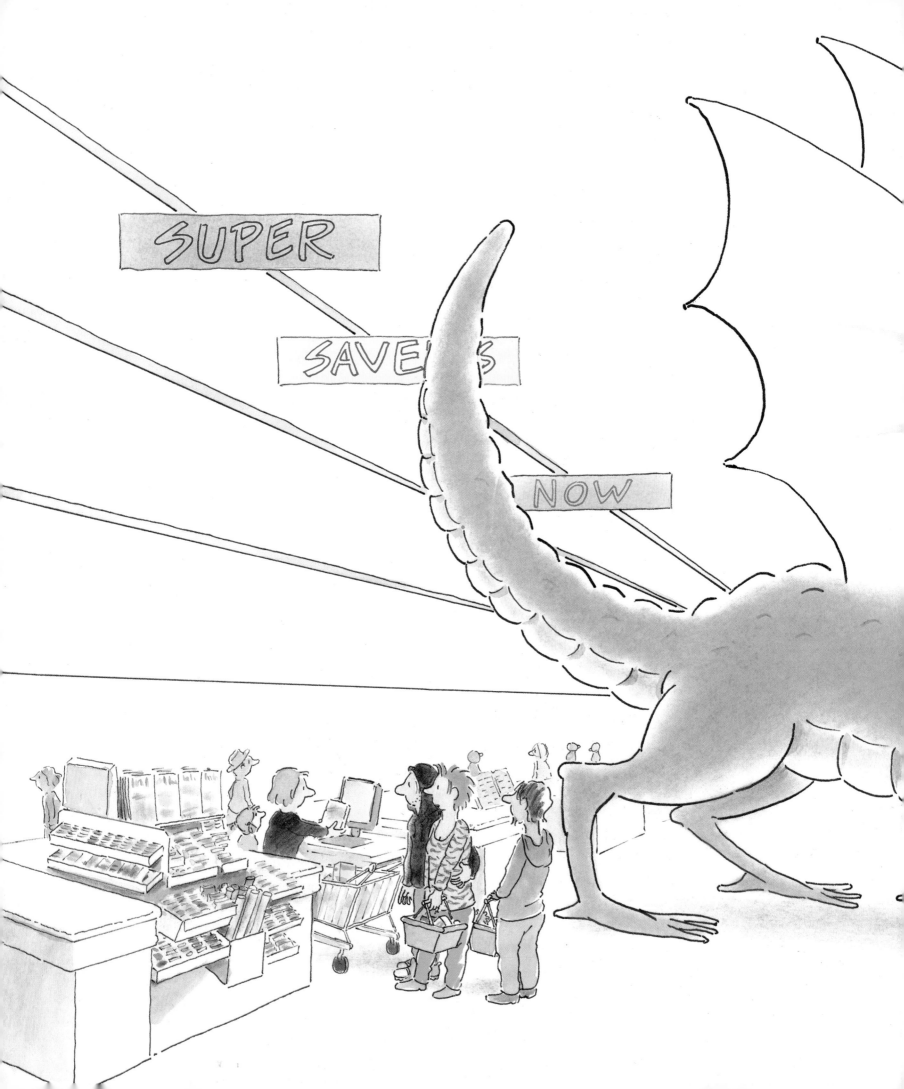